VALISKA GREGORY

A Valentine
for
Norman
Noggs

ILLUSTRATED BY MARSHA WINBORN

HARPERCOLLINSPUBLISHERS

The art in this book was created using watercolor, gouache, colored and pastel pencils, ink, and lace on illustration board.

Library of Congress Cataloging-in-Publication Data

Gregory, Valiska.
    A valentine for Norman Noggs / Valiska Gregory ; illustrated by Marsha Winborn.
        p.   cm.
    Summary: Hamster Norman Noggs hopes to impress the new girl in school on
Valentine's Day but worries because he is not the biggest or the strongest in the class.
    ISBN 0-06-027656-8. — ISBN 0-06-027657-6 (lib. bdg.) — ISBN 0-06-443623-3 (pbk.)
    [1. Valentine's Day—Fiction.   2. Self-esteem—Fiction.   3. Schools—Fiction.
4. Hamsters—Fiction.]   I. Winborn, Marsha, ill.   II. Title.
PZ7.G8624Val   1999   96-48589
[E]—dc21   CIP
                                                                                                  AC

Visit us on the World Wide Web! ❖ http://www.harperchildrens.com

For Eric and his
Wilhemina—Mel
—VG

For Phoebe,
with thanks
—MW

orman Noggs was in love. He sat in the third row, second seat, just behind the new girl in class.

"If I'm lucky," Norman thought, "Wilhemina might turn around and ask me for a pencil." He drew a heart in the margin of his math paper and smoothed his tiny hamster whiskers.

Norman loved the way Wilhemina's eyelashes fluttered like butterflies. He loved the lace on her dress and the buttons on her shiny black shoes.

But Norman Noggs was not the only one who wanted Wilhemina to notice him.

Sigh.

At recess Richard carried two kindergartners across the playground and dropped them right in front of Wilhemina.

"I'm the strongest, toughest person in the whole class," he said.

"Too bad I'm not as tough as Richard," thought Norman. He helped the kindergartners find their way back to their teacher and showed Wilhemina where to line up.

"Thank you," she whispered. Just the sound of Wilhemina's voice made Norman's stomach feel wobbly.

During lunch Arthur ate five pieces of pizza, two helpings of macaroni, and six oatmeal cookies.

"I'm the biggest person in the whole class," he said.

DON'T YOU THINK ARTHUR'S DREAMY?

"Too bad I'm not as big as Arthur," thought Norman.
He showed Wilhemina where to put her tray after lunch.
"Thank you," she said quietly. Looking at Wilhemina's
brown eyes made Norman's knees start to buckle.

That night Norman did twenty-five push-ups and ate two helpings of mashed potatoes. Then he ran around the house until his legs felt like noodles.

He looked in the mirror. His hamster feet looked small in their little red tennis shoes. His ears looked no larger than apple-blossom petals.

"This might take a little time," he said.

MAYBE A LOT OF TIME...

Every day Norman worked hard. He ran from the grocery store to the fire station before breakfast. He ate broccoli and brussels sprouts. He did jumping jacks and somersaults.

Every day he stared at the back of Wilhemina's head and hoped she would turn around.

"I'll bet she doesn't even know my name," he thought. He wrote his name in extra-big letters on his paper, just in case.

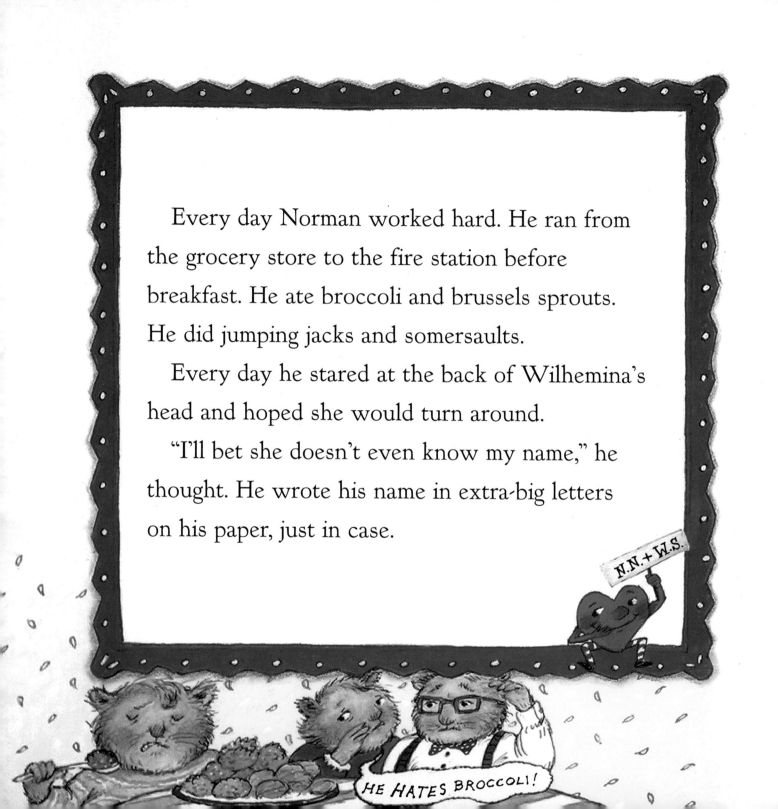

N.N. + W.S.

HE HATES BROCCOLI!

Richard carried Wilhemina's
books to the music room,

and Arthur scored the
most points in gym class.

Norman helped Wilhemina find her blue mitten before
recess and explained the homework in social studies.

"Thank you," she said. Norman felt his insides slide right
down to his socks.

"For Valentine's Day, I'm going to buy Wilhemina the most expensive valentine in the whole world," said Richard.

"But mine is going to be the biggest," said Arthur.

Norman stretched his little neck up to make himself look taller.

"I'm going to make her a valentine with the best words," he said.

"Over my dead body," said Richard.

"Don't even think about it," said Arthur. "Wilhemina isn't going to get any valentines except from us."

Norman thought about what Richard and Arthur might do to him if he gave Wilhemina a valentine. Then he thought about how Wilhemina's cheeks were pink as peppermint drops.

"I'll give a valentine to Wilhemina no matter what," he decided.

He cut out a red heart and glued white paper lace around the edges.

Then he wrote:

Wilhemina
Wilhemina
Won't you be my
Valentine?

Norman tore up his valentine and started over:

Wilhemina is sweet as candy.
Wilhemina is nice as pie.
Wilhemina is just so Dandy
that she makes me
want to sigh.

Norman sighed. He
tore up that heart, too.
   "This is going to be harder than
I thought," he said, "but Wilhemina is worth it."

On Valentine's Day Norman carried his valentine to school. He thought he saw Wilhemina peeking out the window as he walked by her house, but he wasn't sure.

At the corner of the street, blocking his path, stood Richard and Arthur.

"They look big," thought Norman.

Richard growled like a grizzly bear, and Arthur waved his arms like a gorilla.

"They ARE big," Norman decided.

Richard grabbed Norman's valentine and threw it in the gutter. "So much for your valentine," he said. Norman tried walking past, but Arthur grabbed his notebook.

"Look," said Arthur. "He's got another valentine hidden in his notebook."

"I made it just in case something happened to the first one," said Norman.

"Something's going to happen to the second one, too," said Arthur. He tore up the second valentine and stomped the pieces in the snow.

All of a sudden they heard a loud noise.

"*Eeeeeee YAH!*"

said something in a blue coat.
Richard was so surprised, he
slipped on a patch of ice and
went sailing into a mound of snow.

WuFF!!

POW POW

"*Eeeeee* YAH!!"

the blue coat said. Arthur tripped over Richard's sprawling feet.

WOOFF!

WOW!!!

Norman smiled at the person in the blue coat.

"Would you like to walk to school with me?" he asked.

"I'd love to, Norman," said Wilhemina.

"I'm still the toughest," shouted Richard from the snow pile.

"But you're not the smartest," said Wilhemina.

"And I'm still the biggest," yelled Arthur.

"The bigger they are," said Wilhemina, "the harder they fall."

"EeeeeeeYAH," screamed Richard and Arthur.

"Run for it," Wilhemina shouted. Norman grabbed Wilhemina's hand and ran as fast as he could, pulling her along behind him.

They were at their desks before Richard and Arthur had even reached the playground.

Wilhemina turned around and smiled at Norman. "If I teach you karate, will you teach me to run as fast as you can?" she asked.

Norman's tongue wouldn't move at all, so he nodded yes.

"This is for you," said Wilhemina.

Just looking at the envelope made Norman's head feel woozy. He read the valentine:

Dear Norman,

Thanks for being my friend. Will you be my Valentine?

Love,
Wilhemina Stitch

Norman read the valentine twice before he
could believe what it said. Then he unpinned the
third valentine he'd made for Wilhemina from his
shirt sleeve.

The valentine said:

Before handing it to
her, Norman added the
words "strong" and
"smart."

Wilhemina, be my Valentine—Love, here are some words you remind me of: angel flowers dainty stars your friend, norman froggs

He watched as Wilhemina read the valentine, and when
she smiled at him, Norman Noggs blushed like a pink candy
heart.